First Paperback Edition 1995

Text and illustrations copyright © 1994 by Martina Selway

Published by Ideals Children's Books
Nashville, Tennessee

First published in Great Britain by
Hutchinson Children's Books, an imprint of the
Random Century Group, Ltd., London, England

Printed in China.

Library of Congress Cataloging-in-Publication Data

Selway, Martina.
    I hate Roland Roberts/Martina Selway.
        p.   cm.
    Summary: In a letter to her grandfather, Rosie describes her
new school and most especially her new schoolmate, Roland.
    ISBN 0-8249-8660-1 (trade)—ISBN 0-8249-8675-X (pbk.)
    [1. Friendship—Fiction. 2. Schools—Fiction. 3. Letters—
Fiction.] I. Title.
PZ7.S464iah   1994
[E]—dc20   93-30916
                                                          CIP
                                                           AC

I Hate
Roland Roberts

Martina Selway

Ideals Children's Books
Nashville, Tennessee

For Stefan Bandalac

With thanks to the pupils and staff of the
Orchard County First School, East Molesey, Surrey

Rosie has started a new school.
She doesn't like it.
She doesn't like being the new girl.
She doesn't like sitting next to a BOY.
And she does not like Roland Roberts!

1764 Hill Road
Hartford
Connecticut

Dear Grandad,
I hate my new school. It's very big and strange and I don't know anyone. Miss West, the teacher, is all right, but she made me sit next to a BOY named Roland Roberts! At lunchtime she told him to look after me.

Roland Roberts said, "Girls are stupid." Girls are not stupid and I don't want him to look after me.

I hate Roland Roberts!

At recess we all went outside and ran around playing games. Some of the children were so rough that I fell over and scraped my hand. I only cried a little. Roland Roberts said, "It didn't hurt you, crybaby."

It did hurt and I'm not a crybaby.

I hate Roland Roberts.

When Mom came to meet me
after school, she started talking
to Mrs. Roberts. She asked her
to come over one day soon
so that Roland and I could
play together.
Roland Roberts said, "Yuk!"
I made a horrible face. I'm
not playing with HIM.
I hate Roland Roberts.

I took Annabel to school today.
At recess some of the boys ran
off with her and threw her
into the tree. Miss West was
very mad and got her down
with an umbrella.
Roland Roberts said, "It wasn't
us, Miss West."
But I knew it was,
horrible Roland Roberts.

Ugh! Mrs. Roberts and Roland came
over today and I had to take
him to my room to play. I got out
my toy cars and garage.
Roland Roberts said, "I didn't
think silly girls liked cars,
but these old ones are great."
He doesn't know anything,
stupid Roland Roberts.

I was very excited this morning because it had snowed last night. Everything was white all over.
At school everyone was sliding and throwing snowballs. One hit me right on my ear.
Roland Roberts said, "Good shot! Are you all right, Ginge?"
I'm not going to be called Ginge by silly Roland Roberts.

Mom and I went to the park on
Saturday, and we took my sled.
Roland was there with his mom and
dad and their dog, Bran. I had
to share my sled with Roland!
Bran barked and chased us through
the snow. It was fun.
Roland Roberts said, "I wish I had
a sled. Let's make a
snowman tomorrow."
I really like Bran, but
I'm not too sure about Roland Roberts.

We made the biggest, fattest
snowman you ever saw. It was
almost dark when we finished.
I took Mr. Roberts' hat and put it
on top. He called me a little
rascal and pretended to be upset.
Roland Roberts said, "My dad
thinks you're the greatest."
I suppose
he's not so bad, Roland Roberts.

Guess what? Roland's got a pet rat.
His mom lets him keep it in the
kitchen. I had to be very gentle
when I held it because it's
having babies.
Roland Roberts said, "When she has
her babies, you can have one, Ginge."
I've always wanted a pet rat.
He's kind of nice, Roland Roberts.

I showed Roland some photos of me when I stayed on the farm. He's never been on a farm and didn't know that pigs could have thirteen piglets. I told him that I'm going to be a farmer when I grow up.
Roland Roberts said, "So am I. That's what I want to be."
He really likes animals.
I think I like Roland Roberts.

Now we are doing the Christmas play at school. Miss West said that if Roland doesn't behave himself, he won't be Joseph.

Roland Roberts said, "I don't want to be Joseph unless Ginge is Mary."

Can I bring Roland to see you at the farm soon? He's my best friend.

I like Roland Roberts a <u>lot</u>!

Love from
Old Ginger Nut. X

Mr. J. Lee
Griggs Farm
Manchester
Vermont